The Tuuli Function

A novelette by
Steven N. McGannon

For the Students and Staff of
Delta Charter High School
at Cabrillo College —

Everything is possible because of you.

Steven N. McGannon

Author photograph by Austin East
Coloring page illustration by Michael L. McGannon

Acknowledgements

I want to thank Rachel Regelein, whose stimulating conversations always spark fruitful ideas; Michael L. McGannon, both for helping to proofread this story, and for contributing an illustration to serve as its coloring page; and Sally Blumenthal-McGannon, whose discussions and continuing support helped to facilitate bringing this story to publication.

I further want to thank Austin, Matthew, and Lotta—inspiring people who have variously supported, influenced, and contributed in some invaluable way to my career as a writer and to my life at large.

Finally, I am also thankful to the following individuals and organizations: Sean Berben, Ivan Blumberg, Marc Blumberg, Don Blumenthal, Heidi Blumenthal, Randall Bruce, Cindy Chace, Sylvie-Marie Drescher, Shane Hill, AnneMarie Jonasen, Laura McGannon, Alan Segal, Jerry Solomon, the Laukkanen family, all of my Finnish friends and family, all of my Santa Cruz friends and family, Delta Charter High School at Cabrillo College, the wonderful teachers I had at Cabrillo College, my Berkeley friends, and to Bookshop Santa Cruz.

This novelette contains a coloring page.
It is to be found in the pages after the story.
Please feel free to color it, add to it,
or leave it alone in any way that you choose.

1. Tuuli awakens.

2. Tuuli gets out of bed. She looks at her watch. It is 09.45.

3. Tuuli retrieves an iced tea from the fridge.

4. Tuuli locates her backpack in its usual spot next to the front door.

5. Tuuli checks her backpack to be sure that it contains her a) notebook; b) phone; c) wallet; d) keys. She finds that it does.

6. Tuuli enters the bathroom. She showers, she avoids looking in the mirror for the uneasiness of seeing her own eyes staring back at her. She avoids brushing her teeth, and then she exits.

7. Tuuli dresses herself.

    a. She first puts on her underwear,

b. then she puts on a pair of purple shorts,

c. then she puts on a fading cardinal t-shirt,

d. then she puts a neon-yellow basketball sock on each foot,

e. then she puts on a heavy lake-blue jacket,

f. then she puts a chestnut bow in her hair,

g. and finally, she laces up a pair of hiking boots.

8. Tuuli surveys her apartment. She feels as if she has forgotten something. Her head throbs at the temples. She picks up her backpack and holds it with a strap upon her right shoulder while she digs through the front pocket for her keys. She finds them.

9. Tuuli opens the front door, walks through, closes it, and locks it.

10. Tuuli puts her keys back into the front pocket of her backpack, and makes sure that her notebook, phone, and wallet are still there. They are.

11. Tuuli exits the apartment building. She looks at her watch. It is 10.45.

12.   Tuuli walks to the university.

13.   Tuuli arrives at her first class of the day—Early Modern
       Philosophy.

14.   Tuuli, having not read the material for class, listens with
       anxiety. She is not familiar enough with most of the
       material being covered. Boredom pangs her. She can
       learn the material on her own, and she feels that, con-
       sequently, she needs not the lecture.

15.   Tuuli waits. The class seems not to end. She is uncom-
       fortable in her chair. Her lower back is numb. Spinoza
       thinks she and the chair are the same thing.

16.   Tuuli leaves class before it ends. Her watch reads: 11.42.

17.   Tuuli wanders. There is the library. There is the café.
       She walks back and forth between the two.

18.   Tuuli wonders if she will receive a grade that is lower
       than an A on the next assignment. She thinks she will.

19.   Tuuli feels anxious. She checks her watch. It is 12.15.
       She should eat; she should read.

20.   Tuuli begins to head toward the anthropology department. Perhaps, she thinks, someone is there whom she knows—a fellow student.

21.   Tuuli walks up the hill, passes the music department, past the café that is closed for renovation.

22.   Tuuli arrives at the anthropology department.

      a. She walks through the front entrance,

      b. up the stairs,

      c. up the next flight of stairs,

      d. into the hallway,

      e. into the library.

23.   Tuuli looks around. She does not see anyone she knows. She looks at her watch. It is 12.29.

24.   Tuuli feels exasperated and concerned. She tells herself: You should be studying.

25.   Tuuli browses the bookshelves.

26.　Tuuli picks up a book. She likes the artwork on the spine. The book has something to do with archaeology. Archeometry. Archaeology can be so dull, and such busy work, and so unthinking. She puts the book back.

27.　Tuuli frets about the fleeting time. She departs the library.

28.　Tuuli descends the staircases.

29.　Tuuli walks slowly past the café that is being renovated. She stares at her boots as her locomotion propels her along.

30.　Tuuli looks at her watch. It is 12.46.

31.　Tuuli walks past the music department, from which she can almost hear Mozart's requiem jeering at her. She walks down the hill. To her left is the building in which she anticipates her next class will take place. Its many windows frown down upon her.

32.　Tuuli approaches the pursed, disapproving entrance to the building. A student holds the door for her. A vocalization comes softly from Tuuli's throat and through her lips as they open briefly and involuntarily. She did not mean to make the sound. She's caught in convention.

　　She thinks:

a. How stupid you must have sounded.

b. Someone smarter would not make such mistakes.

c. What did they think I meant to say?

d. Why do I do things like this?

e. Why do they hold the door?

f. You don't even read your assigned readings, what are you doing?

g. You are smarter than they are—you are not smarter than they are.

33. Tuuli glances about as she proceeds through the hall-way. She rolls her sleeve up slightly to glimpse the time: It is 12.50.

34. Tuuli wishes for the panacea.

35. Tuuli sits next to the doorway to her next class. Room 105. Class will begin soon.

36. Tuuli is uncomfortable on the hard surface of the floor—her back hurts pressed down with her own weight atop her.

37. Tuuli checks her watch. It is 12.55. She pushes herself up from the floor and stands on her tiptoes to peer through the small, square glass pane of the door to see if there is a class currently underway. There is. She sits back down.

38. Tuuli watches as the door opens. Students exit.

39. Tuuli pushes herself up again and waits until most of the room has been drained. She enters and sits in back.

40. Tuuli arches her back. She looks about. No one else has yet entered for the next class: Philosophy of David Hume.

41. Tuuli wonders what her fellow students think of her.

42. Tuuli observes her fellow students begin to arrive. She wonders if she has the appearance of a dandizette or a wench. Maybe even something else?

43. Tuuli glances at her watch once again. It is 13.01. The day seems to stretch. It feels to her as if there is more

of it between 11.00 and 14.00 than there is at any other 3-hour interval.

44. Tuuli scribbles logic proofs on her notebook. They are rudimentary—she has never taken a logic course. She knows little of them, but she admires the way they look.

45. Tuuli wonders what scribbles she would make if she had taken a logic course or two. Maybe more boxes? Other shapes?

46. Tuuli sees the professor walk in. She becomes anxious. For a moment, her clock beats faster.

47. Tuuli stares at her watch. It is 13.07. Then it is 13.08.

48. Tuuli pens a dash for each time the second hand moves.

49. Tuuli notices that it is now 13.09.

50. Tuuli hears the voice of the lecturer begin to drone. She has not completed the reading for this class session either. She is concerned in this regard. She wishes she would read.

51. Tuuli listens. She wonders what grade she will receive on the quiz that she recently submitted online. Hume thinks she can't justify any reason for thinking she will receive *any* grade on the quiz. A comforting thought.

52. Tuuli wonders about what Hume might have thought about what the professor was saying about the *Treatise* these few hundred years after its publication. Perhaps he would better understand what he had written.

53. Tuuli finds this class more interesting than the other ones. It still doesn't incline her toward the readings.

54. Tuuli hopes that class will soon end. She thinks:

    a. This is boring—

    b. this is interesting.

    c. This is the kind of thing I want to know.

    d. I can read this on my own; I can learn this on my own.

    e. Humans have thought such interesting thoughts.

    f. Do I think interesting thoughts?

    g. How can I tell if I think interesting thoughts?

    h. Is it enough that they interest me?

    i. Do they interest me? Can I answer this? Am I interested? If I am, then I should consider them as interesting to me. Does that follow? Perhaps I should write it down. Will it be clearer if it is written down? What is clarity? How do I make it clear? How do I make things clear? Do I seem to? May I? Can I? Am I capable of this?

55.   Tuuli hears the chirp of a bird beyond the window. She wonders if it was a bird that in fact produced it. Could it not have been? The question is silly.

56.   Tuuli thinks: I have forgotten what I was going to write down. What was it? I have such a terrible memory. If I had a better memory people would think that I am smarter than they currently do.

    She thinks: Well of course they would… wouldn't anyone be smarter if they had a better memory than they do? They might certainly appear to be. Is there anything to smartness beyond the appearance of smartness? Surely. How? How does this work?

    She thinks: Is memory some fundamental component of intelligence? Well of course, but to what extent? Well, I can't know that; Wittgenstein wouldn't have worried about that.

    She thinks: What was I thinking? What am I missing? It is like the test where you arrange colored blocks into given shapes, but then there's a shape you can't figure out and you realize you've stumbled and you get anxious, and the anxiety makes you worse, and then everything falls apart. I can't see the shape. I can't arrange the blocks. Can someone? Does someone see all the shapes? At least they picked you to take the test.

57. Tuuli looks at her watch. The hour-hand is beyond the number 1; the minute-hand is beyond the number 7; the second-hand ticks 1 unit beyond the 5. Hume thinks Tuuli doesn't have an impression of time.

58. Tuuli wonders what Hume would have thought of her. How strange it would be if Hume—the person—actualized in front of her, came out from the evaporation of whatever pieces or piece had made him up when he had been alive. There in his orange coat thing he would speak with a surprised, archaic Scottish accent about the glowing tablets upon which many fellow students' fingers would pace.

59. Tuuli thinks that her thoughts are too metaphorical.

60. Tuuli remembers that she has known other people who spoke more metaphorically than her thoughts think. This doesn't mean her thoughts are not too metaphorical. But at least, she thinks, they aren't completely out the window.

61.   Tuuli presses a finger against her cheek. She wonders if anyone else is watching her.

62.   Tuuli looks at her watch. It is 13.50. Finally, class nears its end.

63.   Tuuli wonders if she can just leave now. She supposes that she had better wait until 13.54. That seems a reasonable time. It will appear as if she has something urgent to get to—she hopes.

64.   Tuuli quietly shuffles her notebook into her backpack. She glances 'round. It is time to leave.

65.   Tuuli stands, walks, exits the classroom. The door sounds behind her. The teacher's back had been turned. What he must think of her.

66.   Tuuli breathes relievedly. She is glad to be rid of the classes for the day.

67.   Tuuli resumes fretting about the severe paucity of reading she has been doing. There are only a couple weeks left in the semester. She doesn't want to know exactly how many…there are not enough.

68.   Tuuli begins to amble back in the general direction of her apartment. Wretched place.

69.   Tuuli feels tired. Her head is warm. She wonders why she feels tired everyday around this time. She thinks: This is why I can't do my reading—I am too tired. This is so burdensome. If I were less tired people would think that I am smarter; that I am not this disheveled wretch.

70.   Tuuli is annoyed with herself. This is not unusual for her.

71.   Tuuli steps forward with one foot, then the next. Each step isn't so different, but she will eventually reach her apartment. Unless it is no longer there—she thinks.

72.   Tuuli passes:

    a. Under the gate,

    b. through the square,

    c. over the crosswalk,

    d. by the storefront,

        d.1. by the next storefront,

        d.2. by the storefront after that,

d.3. by the storefront after that,

d.4. by the storefront after that,

d.5. by the storefront after that,

d.6. by the storefront after that,

d.7. by the storefront after that,

e. the corner restaurant,

f. the street's bend,

g. down the street,

h. the houses left and right,

i. the stray cats on the stray couches,

j. fellow students with their friends,

k. further crosswalks and their crossers,

l. under trees,

m. over—and not on—cracks in the cement,

n. by the last apartment building prior to hers,

o. 'round the cars in the driveway,

p. up and over each stair,

q. through the doorframe of the apartment building,

r. by the railing up the stairs,

s. through her front door,

t. the trash on the way to the couch.

73. Tuuli sits down upon the couch. She feels her eyes ache, her back strain, her body crumble beneath her own existence. She thinks: O, how continental.

74. Tuuli lies down. Her knees ache. She closes her eyes. Her brow throbs. She is a burden.

75. Tuuli imagines her walk back to the apartment in the reverse. It must be 14.15 by now. Class had ended. What if she had stayed? Would it have helped?

76. Tuuli thinks about how boring everything is. She wishes she had something to do. She thinks: You should read. She thinks: I am too tired.

77.   Tuuli tries not to think. She looks at the back of her eye-
       lids and sees blackness. But then she notices that she
       sees colors. Many strings of vaguely neon colors—
       yellow, blue, red...is this what blackness looks like? she
       wonders. Does blackness consist in anything else? They
       say it does, she imagines. She doesn't know. She sees
       color.

78.   Tuuli imagines a rainbow. Sateenkaari. Are rainbows
       the origin of all religion? Newton thinks about rain-
       bows. *Thought*—she thinks she should have thought.
       Spectrums. Spectra.

79.   Tuuli thinks about words that sound similar. She doesn't
       immediately think of any word that sounds like rain-
       bow. She worries. What is she doing? Her eyes are closed
       tightly, but some light filters through. Her lids look red.
       Is it blood or light that she sees? she wonders.

80.   Tuuli is like a rainbow. She wishes this were so. She
       gravitates towards rainbows. She is colorful; she has
       color. She thinks: Maybe you should try rainbow sorbet.

81.   Tuuli is frustrated with herself. There is nothing to her
       thoughts. She should be smarter than this—she thinks.
       But why? she wonders.
            She thinks: Am I really better at wondering than
       answering? Am I worse at arguing than wondering? Is

wondering good for anything on its own? Does it need to be? Why would I even think this in the first place? Other people must wonder more interesting things. I wonder what Wittgenstein wondered. Would he have wondered what I wonder? Or would he wonder about what he wondered? That doesn't sound like him. Then again, you don't know him. Even if you had, would that have helped you answer your question? What was your question? Why do I think *you* instead of *me* when it is me that is doing the thinking? Is this an aspect of language that constructs my reality? Would I refer to *your reality* if it wasn't my reality of which I was thinking? Can I say "thinking of"? Why must it be "of which"? It mustn't. But that isn't so because *mustn't* means *must not*, and it isn't imperative that it must not, rather it just doesn't seem to need to. Am I confusing what *imperative* should mean? Someone smarter than I would know. And who would that be? Why do my thoughts sound like—*think* like questions? The question mark. I need a wonder mark. What's the difference? Well, the imploration, certainly. Right? Wonder doesn't implore you to suss out a definite answer. *Wonder* might be said to be kaleidoscopic rather than microscopic or telescopic. Is that a helpful metaphor? You should sleep. Read or sleep.

82. Tuuli returns to looking at the back of her eyelids. She looks too intently to lose focus and fall asleep.

83.   Tuuli wants to dream of rainbows. She has become infatuated with them recently.

84.   Tuuli wonders if she would have been better off studying physics or mathematics. She would know then whether she could do something or not. It would be obvious. It would be given.

85.   Tuuli thinks about particular actions she has carried out. Sometimes, she makes up simple algebraic functions because she likes to wonder (aimlessly) how they work. If you follow the rules, the steps, and input the same number, you will always get the same result. What kind of thing is this? She wonders if she is just a function. She wonders if things are just a function of her. The Tuuli Function. What would that look like? $x(Tuuli)$; $Tuuli(x)$… something. Tuuli*(table)*; *Tuuli(chair)*; *Tuuli(sorrow)*; *Tuuli(despondence)*. Is she a predicate, rather? Or more like code maybe. She thinks: Maybe I'm a machine—a Turing machine. Then why this cumbersome biology? A stupid machine.

86.   Tuuli wonders if forming questions is not simply a manner of disguising a lack of creativity in answer-crafting. It doesn't matter what the answer is to that, however, because either way she can only seem to ask questions and not answer them. She needs the wonder mark.

87.   Tuuli is now quite fed-up with herself. Sleep! she commands.

88.   Tuuli wishes she would sleep.

89.   Tuuli lifts an eyelid. She situates her wrist such that the watch face atop it faces her. Her muscles contract. The clock reads: 14.37.

90.   Tuuli closes her eyes. She moans softly. How much of the day will be wasted sleeping? Her dreams are more lively and vivacious in the daytime. She has work to do.

91.   Tuuli considers the rainbow. It's an optical thing. It is composed of colors. Well, technically it is composed of something like the refractive dispersion of light through water droplets…or reflection or something. But it looks colored. It is experienced as color. Simple color. It spreads into an arc. Or it is seen as an arc, typically. God makes rainbows some people think.

92.   Tuuli isn't Joan-like in *that* arcian respect, but she does fancy rainbows.
      At the bottom, purple begins, posed over a sensible background, and somewhere vague this purple becomes blue, and somewhere vague this blue becomes green, and somewhere vague this green becomes yellow, and somewhere vague this yellow becomes orange, and

somewhere vague this orange becomes red, and somewhere vague this red ends.

93.   Tuuli thinks again of nothing. She holds nothing. She
       thinks of rainbows.

94.   Tuuli thinks of rainwater plopping down upon a cement
       surface.

95.   Tuuli thinks of rainwater.

96.   Tuuli thinks of rain.

97.   Tuuli thinks.

...Hallways can be quiet. This one is. There isn't anyone around. There are bookshelves. Every book looks
like it has life. They all look like they are looking at me.
I want to read them all. I want to know every word
each one says. I want to have read them. It would take
so long to read them all. I don't want to read them all.
I want to have read them. There are people I know.
How did they arrive here? This is my library. This is my
head. How can I think of other people? Is it other
people I am thinking of? —of whom I am thinking?
They probably don't understand what I am like inside.
Neither do I. Shallow. Hollow.
    There is Maiju—I haven't seen her in so long. She is

speaking. Behold what perspicacity! Her mouth moves; she says things; she is beautiful; she is pataphorical; she knows things; she thinks well; I don't like her; she is stupid; she knows more than I do; I don't like that; I don't like myself; I wish I liked myself; if I were her I'd like myself; but then I'd like her; I already like her; I wonder if she likes me; What is she saying I haven't been paying attention My thoughts are moving too quickly for that sort of thing I forgot her name the first 5 times she told me I was embarrassed She embarrasses me with her intelligence I am smarter than her She can't think the things I think Well that is so in conception Can she think things better than I do I wonder what it is like to think like her What does she know that I don't know What does she see that I don't see What is it to be in her world What do things look like Do her thoughts move faster Does she reach conclusions faster Or does she simply have better ideas intrinsically It can't be that way though—she understands that all intelligence amounts to is the particular timbre of your bafflement, or does she? Does it? She can spell well, her vocabulary is good, mine isn't But surely I am better at some things Or one thing Does that make it worthwhile? Does it matter that some are better at some things? What if she is better at everything, strictly better Am I still valuable? Of course you are, but why? She doesn't need to rely on being afterwise. It comes as effortless for her to disarm the people she meets.

Maiju's mouth moves, she says more things. She knows things I do not know. Do I know anything she doesn't? She says she likes me...is this so? Does she admire my mind? If so, why? What about it? Or does she politely, conventionally, treat me as other people are so enforced to do by the trappings of their respective cultures? Which would be worse? Is there any option that is preferable? Do I have a preference? What is it to have a preference? Does she have a preference? Can I just watch myself without participating? Can't I just be another atom determined to bump around? But Leibniz thinks I am a monad—I don't "bump" around now, do I? With no windows to see out of you'd think I'd hit something eventually…

98. Tuuli awakens. No more rainbows. She thinks: You dream about her. Why? You're stupid.

99. Tuuli peers at her watch's face. It is 16.01. She has slept.

100. Tuuli does not want to be awake. She doesn't like her dreams. She wonders why she thinks about Maiju so often. It seems unfair that even in dreams she cannot escape.

101. Tuuli considers how strange her dreams are. Fragmentary things; images; scenes. They move quickly from one to another, in between there are black gaps in the midst of which it feels like nothing to exist. She dreams less at nighttime. There isn't much discerning between a dream and a memory, for Tuuli.

102. Tuuli has a piercing headache. She moves her head. It hurts her. The ache in her head itself is uncomfortable. It would rather be in another head. Tuuli wonders what it would be like for this thought to be the case.

   "Tuuli," she says to herself, prodding her nose, "Do you hear the blood rushing through your head? Yes. Does it make you feel bleak? Yes." She hates it. This is what she is—the kind of thing that has blood, whose blood is pumped, and who is bound to operate via valves.

103. Tuuli wonders why she is ever wrong. She wonders why she writes a sentence with an error in it. What is the nature of the error? she wonders. Why is it an error? she wonders. Is it proper to call it an error? Why do I have to make them? she wonders these things. Perhaps it's the valves?

104. Tuuli thinks about her assignments. One of them is due quite soon.

105. Tuuli knows she should arise from the couch and work on something. She does not. She does not want to.

106. Tuuli is hungry. She lies motionless, save for her heaving chest, upon the couch, wrapped in her own arms, holding the same position as that in which she fell asleep thinking about rainbows. She thinks: Was it rainbows?

I have forgotten. She thinks: I can't believe I went to class earlier today. She thinks: If I could only delineate timeframes better internally I would be smarter, I would know more, I would have more time and motivation and energy to study.

107. Tuuli hoists herself up into a sitting position. She is steadfast—more than that, she has *sisu*.

108. Tuuli sits upon the couch. This is an achievement. Her body moans. Her skeleton creaks beneath the weight of her muscles. Her nerve endings tingle. She feels her gangly arms and legs protruding oddly from whatever stocky thing she happens to be.

109. Tuuli feels strange. She feels out-of-place.

110. Tuuli looks at her watch again. It's 16.20.

111. Tuuli tells herself: It's alright—you've got plenty of time. You don't need to start for hours. You can finish your paper if you start even as late as 22.00.

       She thinks: No, that's too late. Start by a minimum of 20.30. You need an A on this.

       She thinks: Maximum?

112. Tuuli tells herself she is a competent writer. Then she reminds herself that she hasn't read the material. Can your writing save you, Tuuli? she wonders.

113. Tuuli wonders if all she can ever do is wonder. Maybe the system looks something like:
Input (x) → *Tuuli* → *Output (wonder about x)*

114. Tuuli wonders if she will ever feel differently.

115. Tuuli feels restless. She lifts the remote for the TV from its resting spot on the stool in front of the couch.

116. Tuuli presses the maroon oval "power" button.

117. Tuuli wonders what she should watch. She tries to ignore the nagging thought of all of the work that needs to be done. There's more now than there was a few hours ago. It multiplies.

118. Tuuli decides to watch *Tulitikkutehtaan tyttö*. It is her favorite film. Buttons work under her fingers. The images appear on the screen.

119. Tuuli watches as scenes follow successively. Somehow, the film passes by.

120. Tuuli, at some time, notices abruptly that the film has ended.

121. Tuuli wonders if she should listen to music.

122. Tuuli thinks: I want to listen to music, and this seems to be a sufficient reason to put some on.

123. Tuuli stirs from her seated couch position. She moves toward her record player. She picks records. She wonders what she wants to listen to. She wonders if she should know before she puts it on or if she should put it on and then discover whether she wants to listen to it or not.

124. Tuuli lies on the carpet and listens to:

    a. Elliott Smith,

    b. Pinback,

    c. The Beatles,

    d. the sounds of her neighbor moving furniture or something,

    e. Procol Harum,

    f. *Almoraima,*

    g. Chopin's "Scherzo #1 in B minor, Op. 20, B 65,"

    h. Brahms' "Scherzo in E-flat minor, Op. 4,"

    i. Sibelius' "Karelia Suite, Op. 11,"

    j. silence.

125. Tuuli feels things when she listens to music that she doesn't feel when she doesn't listen to music. She really *feels*. She feels like she can understand what people mean when they talk about how they feel "in their heart." It means the same thing as a melody. She wouldn't remember the precise names of the scherzos if she didn't have the album sleeve to examine.

126. Tuuli realizes that she has been listening to music and feeling things for a long time. She abhors her watch. It's 18.15.

127. Tuuli wonders how it got so late. She thinks it's because she's been wasting time. She knows, however, that at some point it would have gotten late anyway.

128. Tuuli frets about the insurmountable pile of work she must now suffer under.

129. Tuuli tries to imagine what life would be like outside of university. She can't picture it. No picture arises in her mind. Only the words, "Life after university," string together in her mind. They attach to nothing. They picture nothing. Does her language fail? she wonders.

130. Tuuli stands.

131. Tuuli paces.

132. Tuuli wonders how she can persist through all of this. She wonders how it is possible that she could still exist after all these thoughts, thoughts that jostle her so vigorously. She wonders how much longer she will persist. She wonders what persisting is. She wonders what she consists in. She wonders how inconsistent she is.

133. Tuuli becomes aggravated with herself. She wants to stop thinking. Her thoughts aggravate her. She wonders if she aggravates other people. Is this the word that best describes her personhood?

134. Tuuli thinks she should try to relax. She thinks she should be gentler. She thinks: Why are you so hostile? What makes you so volatile? She thinks: Don't think that—that's what you shouldn't think! She thinks: Don't be so self-critical, that's really what you shouldn't do.

She thinks: No, this is what I should stop—arguing with myself, internecine. She thinks: Stop. Just stop it.

135.   Tuuli sits down on the couch again.

136.   Tuuli wonders what would be soothing. What would being *soothed* be like?

137.   Tuuli thinks: Music, music…something. Well of course! "When Day is Done" by Django Reinhardt—that is soothing!

138.   Tuuli hops up from the couch. She rushes to her record player. She fumbles through records. She finds Django. She balances the record upon the turntable. It rests flat. She turns the nob. She lifts the needle. She places the needle quite accurately. The speakers emit crackling sounds, and then the jangling begins.

139.   Tuuli returns to the couch. She smiles. She lies down. She stretches her legs. For a fleeting moment she is tranquil.

140.   Tuuli, yet, is struck rapidly with anxiety. She has not even begun to read her assignments. What is she writing about? Parmenides? Thales? Epicurus? Greek people? No…a different course.

141.   Tuuli lets the Django Reinhardt record play. It spins around. She doesn't want to turn it off. She feels she must finally get started on her essay. Where has her computer gone? she wonders. The question implores an answer. Aha! She thinks: This I *can* answer!

142.   Tuuli looks about her. Her eyes flutter.

143.   Tuuli sees the edge of her computer. It is lying under a stack of old papers, a bitter gallimaufry of essays, handouts, exams, quizzes, notes, book pages, and ink splotches.

144.   Tuuli recoils at the sight of the computer. It reminds her that on its hard drive sits the absence of the essay she is supposed to have finished by tomorrow. She hesitates.

145.   Tuuli overcomes herself and extracts the electronic thing gingerly out from underneath the pile of slop. She holds it at arm's length.

146.   Tuuli steps back to the couch. She sits. She frowns. She opens the computer. The screen brightens. *Fate of the Animals* stares back at her from her desktop. She wonders what Franz Marc would have written about Xenophanes. She thinks: What would I have written about Franz Marc? What would Voltaire have written about him? What would Voltaire have written about me? But

now you've gone too far. What would I have written about Voltairine de Cleyre? A pamphlet? A poem? A rhyme?

> *Voltairine de Cleyre,*
> *adjectives beware!*
> *You can find her works at any decent anarchist book fair...*

Dreadful. You can't write poetry...Perhaps nursery rhymes? Refocus.

147. Tuuli slips her lengthy finger across the track pad. The mouse on the screen moves. She opens a blank document. This is the formidable page on which she hopes to compose something that will get her a decent grade.

148. Tuuli bites her lip. She looks to the upper right of her computer's screen. The time is nearly 19.00.

149. Tuuli types words. She types what she remembers. Her words are in English. She stares at them carefully. If she rearranged some of the letters the words would be in Finnish. Suomen kieli. She'd like that. She'd like to proclaim: "Opiskelen filosofiaa!" Mutta hän ei puhu suomea.

150. Tuuli deletes. She retypes. She winces. She finds this boring. She struggles. She looks at the time: 4 minutes have passed. She stops. She is tired.

151. Tuuli closes her computer.

152. Tuuli places her computer on the floor and turns her back on it. She huddles on the couch. She feels as if she might unravel.

153. Tuuli lies down. She closes her eyes. She is so tired. Her mind floats about, clanging up against the inside of her skull.

154. Tuuli imagines a meadow. It is a vast expanse, with lush, long, fertile green grass blades and billowing blue skies that stretch up toward the faint surface of the daytime moon. There are flowers with strawberry petals wavering in the lulling breeze, dotting about the low slopes of the endless hills. There is one tree, a tall, sturdy, stern birch. Its branches stretch beyond view, and shield Tuuli's eyes from direct sunbeams. She would prefer to be here. She wouldn't mind dying underneath that tree. Any day now.

155. Tuuli opens her eyes. In front of her is the same stagnant and still room. Her apartment. It is filled with trash. She hates it.

156. Tuuli wonders why the world in her head won't manifest into something actual. She wants to be on her make-believe meadow. The only thing missing from it was a rainbow.

157. Tuuli asks herself: Why can't there be a rainbow?

158. Tuuli once again shuts her eyes. She imagines the meadow again, the very same one, but this time she pictures some boat-sail clouds perspiring just enough so as to take the sun rays struck through them and produce in vibrant hues. There was the rainbow, arcing across the sky.

159. Tuuli thinks: Why are you so stupid? What would Maiju think? What would anyone else think? You deserve to fail. You are a failure. You cannot do anything. Everything you do is awful. All you can think about is made up rainbows and meadows and stupid things.

160. Tuuli stares blankly up at the enormous Finnish flag hung over her couch.

161. Tuuli purses her lips. She frowns. She thinks: Siniristilippu. She wishes she were in Finland. Suomi. What are the Finnish rainbows like? she wonders.

    Sateenkaaren värit: violetti, sininen, vihreä, keltainen, oranssi, ja punainen.

That's the best she could do.

162. Tuuli sighs. Even optimistically, she couldn't be more than ≈0.03% composed of Finnish words.

163. Tuuli yearns for the purple flavors of mustikkakeitto.

164. Tuuli shudders at the touch of her own skin. She has moved her legs slightly. Her left foot has gone numb. The anxiety has mounted within her chest. Her heart flutters. She feels as if her chest is itself a tightly clenched fist. She dares not look at her watch.

165. Tuuli gasps for breath. Her throat hurts terribly. She must look at her watch. She does. It is approximately 19.30. Succession, or maybe, expansion, steadily unfolds.

166. Tuuli thinks about her situation—which, she revises, is rather more aptly described as a *predicament*.

167. Tuuli thinks: Why can't it be the beginning of the semester? If it were, I would have time to do the readings, I would keep up with the assignments, I would be in a much better position. But then, she thinks, near the end of every semester she thinks these same things. She never does anything radically differently.

168. Tuuli lightly smacks herself in the head. If you were smarter, she scolds herself, you would have had indigo and violet in your rainbows instead of purple. Newton did.

169. Tuuli wants to go back to sleep. She feels so tired.

170. Tuuli considers taking some medication. Any benzo-diazepines would do. Besides clonazepam. She shud-ders. Perhaps such things would calm her down and help her work. She shudders again. Imagine what such things did to her brain. It was difficult enough to imagine that greyish tangle sitting there in her skull directing her biology at all. What must it think of her?

171. Tuuli winces at the thought of her thoughts confined within her biology, banging up against the walls. But her thoughts just are her biology. What is it doing to make these thoughts? she wonders. She wishes it wouldn't do whatever that thing is that it does. Any other world would be preferable.

172. Tuuli thinks: What are you doing? You're running out of time. Overcome yourself. You have to work. You are a machine. You are a computer. You are 1s and 0s. You are an automaton. Your circuits whir. Do what other biological stuffs cannot do—overcome yourself.

173. Tuuli harshly slaps her own face several times. She stands simultaneous to the final impact.

174. Tuuli heads into the kitchen. She thinks: Disgusting place.

175. Tuuli with a grimace on her face opens the fridge. The light hurts her squinted eyes.

176. Tuuli extracts an iced tea. She has had so many in the past week. Her heart flutters.

177. Tuuli slams the fridge and drinks from the bottle as she heads back towards the couch.

    Tuuli thinks: Maiju says *toward*; I say *towards*. Annoying. What if she thinks that I'm just like everyone else? Who cares what she thinks. You were the writing prodigy. Be sincere. Be humble. What are you saying? You can't even get through 10 words of your assignments. That's your capability—no one constrains you. But that's different; you know you're different from most people. That means nothing if the product is the same. I hate myself. Maybe you're just exactly the same.

178. Tuuli clutches at her chest. The iced tea's flavor is over-familiar. Her heart flutters. She feels hollow inside.

179. Tuuli wonders what she is, what she is good for, what her function is. She wishes she could watch herself without participating.

180. Tuuli considers asking someone for help with organizing her schedule. She thinks: If I only had just a bit of help keeping my notes straight and my deadlines in order. Just a little. She thinks: No. If you even require help you have failed. That you have thought about this as an option is a sign of sure ineptitude. What can you accomplish thinking this way? You have to overcome yourself. You can. You have to.

181. Tuuli puts down her iced tea. She opens her computer again. The nearly empty document stares back at her. The sight of what is written on it is more painful to endure than the sight of any blank page. It is the worst thing she has ever written.

182. Tuuli wonders what Maiju would do in her situation. She thinks: Obviously, the same thing I would.

183. Tuuli suffers. Anguish. Her body shudders. She feels her heart thump beyond her control. For the time being she despises whomever it is who is responsible for creating the institution of the university. Plato? Aristotle? Someone else? She wasn't sure.

184. Tuuli once again snaps her computer shut. She decides that it doesn't matter what time it is, though she looks anyway, and she sees that it is 19.57.

185. Tuuli distracts herself with her records. She stares at their folds. She thumbs through their cardboard. The Beatles. She likes The Beatles. She likes them more than just about anything else of any kind. They sing about love. She likes love. She thinks: Simone Weil doesn't like love. Nobody reads Simone Weil.

186. Tuuli wonders what Wittgenstein would have thought about The Beatles. They were definitely outside the box. Of course, Bertrand Russell met Paul McCartney… or should it be, "Paul McCartney met Bertrand Russell"? Tuuli supposes that the answer to this depends upon the manner in which you weigh philosophy and music.

187. Tuuli sits cross-legged and muses about the wonderful decade of the 1960s—which she missed. She had to exist all these years later, years where philosophy mattered even less and anxiety was somehow even more prevalent. Some cosmic be-in *this* is. Although, she reckoned, she'da probably not done too well in any era, doomed always to be whatever it is she is.

188. Tuuli looks back at her records and puzzles over what she should listen to. She knows she should work; read;

do stuff. She picks up *The Don Killuminati: The 7 Day Theory*. She imagines that those who know her, the few, wouldn't guess she actually, sincerely, liked this album. And why not? she wondered.

189. Tuuli listens to the songs play. She wonders if her voice is husky. It pleases her to think so.

190. Tuuli wonders why Tupac isn't studied in philosophy. What is less philosophical about the things he says than those philosophers of the proper canon? For that matter, why aren't other artists? Why isn't Jean Sibelius? Why isn't Aleksis Kivi? Or Eero Järnefelt? Or Minna Canth? Isn't the world filtered through them as well? Isn't what results from that filtering what we call philosophy? Or is it a formal thing? It is the format. That could be a part of it, Tuuli supposes. And not *every* artist has to be Tupac or Finnish either.

191. Tuuli thinks: There's nothing about Tupac that Wittgenstein wouldn't like. What the hell does that mean? I don't know, but it sounds interesting. It's not enough for it to sound interesting; it needs to have some substantive content. Think of Maiju. She would have something of substantive content to think. Do better, be better. Substantive. Ampliative. Improve yourself. I wish that my biology would mutate into something more interesting. Just a bit smarter, a bit faster, a bit quicker,

a bit sharper, a bit brighter, more brilliant, more intense, more profound. Say better things, write better ways, retain more information. 1s and 0s, 1s and 0s. Work. Synthesize. Be like those art critics who are actually good, the ones who are so insightful they somehow make their profession seem worthwhile. That's not nice, they are smart too, I'm sure. How can I improve? Several points on the intelligence test? Nobody in possession of an earnest intelligence pays attention to those tests—you know that; don't be stupid. Don't be stupid…it's a threshold thing anyway.

192. Tuuli thinks about how deeply she hates herself at the moment. That's a fairly deep well to fall down. Yet, she figured, it was just as well to fall down it.

193. Tuuli wonders why it must be such a struggle. It is such a struggle to type, and the struggle amounts to a kind of suffering. Admittedly, it is a selfish kind of suffering. If retrospect continually provides information on how to avoid the particular type of recurrent suffering that so ailed Tuuli, perhaps she could take heed from such a trove of experience and act to disrupt the repetition (thereby ending the suffering). Tuuli would rather it be that she could opt out of participation and just watch herself act. This cannot be, Tuuli.

194. Tuuli checks the watch again. It's a later time than it was before. It's a closer time to a less-than-A grade.

195. Tuuli imagines that her mind must be turning to mush. A thinking mush. A glob. This is just the kind of thing brains are. Tuuli thinks: *The kind of thing such and such is* sure sounds like the kind of thing a trained philosophy student says to earn treats. This is what training does—it exorcises every hopeful blossom of creativity that ignited the interest in the object of study that the study of the object purported to be a study about. Yet that doesn't matter; Tuuli thinks: You still have an essay to write.

196. Tuuli knows that it's 20.30. The record has spun to a halt. Tuuli is on the couch. It has reached the time where her thoughts begin to mix together. One word commences and another finishes. Thais'owts going-togo now yew'aited toloong. They're slower, disjunctive, lazier. Sips of iced tea, caffeine—rub water on your face, rub your eyes and your temples, precisify, manifest mental acuity.

197. Tuuli scolds herself. She picks up her exiled computer. This will be the time she writes. The words are gonna go on. The keyboard—there's going to be an essay. But, Tuuli recalls, if I knew anything I'd have already written it. How old are you? You're losing the time.

Think of Hume, think of Ramsey, think of Saul Kripke. Un-age and have actual talent at something, hmm?

Tuuli thinks: Perhaps I should actually get some sort of help with how to structure my time. There must be some support or something the university provides. For what? you moron. For thinking? Everybody thinks; everyone has a hard time; no one wants to write boring papers. But *that* I find them boring, that is the problem. You just said the problem was—wait what did I say? I thought it—not *said* it. Who cares? This has to be ab-normal. This thinking can't be the usual way. Can it? It's as if I am talking to someone else while knowing that it is me. I don't understand. Is there anything beneficial about this? But people do think I am good at some things. I know they do. But what? And why? What am I good for? Shut up—write the essay. I can't; I don't want to; I won't. Then you'll get 0—an F. And you think grades are relevant? Wittgenstein didn't get any Fs. You don't know that. Why would he? He was actually good at things. So are you. Not that good. Maybe. Doubtful. Possibly. Doubtful. Hopefully. Could I be? Are other people? Does it matter? What does the comparison mean? Whatever the answer, what could the answer mean? Nothing important.

198. Tuuli briefly considers George Berkeley and his less-than-deferential analysis of infinitesimals. This is the alleged topic of her imminent essay.

199. Tuuli thinks about "The Philosopher" off *Human* by Death. Good album. She can hear each note; she could play each note.

200. Tuuli thinks about her fellow students. They are all so good at things. Or rather, they are each very good at at least one thing. They have purpose. They are purposeful in some, relevant respect. Their actions seem to have some sort of coherence, some reasonable course. They have sense. They have meaning. They can use words to communicate.

201. Tuuli wonders: What is it about a person that inso-having, as such, gives them a course? What provides them with actions that follow? Why can't I figure that out? Why don't I have that? Is it like causation? Is it an interpretation of sequence? Am I bound to notice succession, and, is succession all that my thinking they have teleology amounts to? I hope that it is. Perhaps they are as desolate as I am. Is it recognition that causes me trouble? Is some internal, psychological reflection on my own circumstance what makes me so fragile?— and volatile?—and hopeless?

202. Tuuli feels that she is going nowhere. Why can't I be like everyone else? Just determined to do as they do. Yet I am so, it must be this way. If I accept that they are determined, then I surely am subject to this same

ease. I should be at ease with being. It's subjectivity—
that's what curses me. *That* I have to notice my participation in this mess. I don't know what it would mean
to say that I wish I had never existed—I can't make
sense of this statement with any precision—but I do
feel this way, and in so feeling…it's the best I can do.

203. Tuuli struggles, anxiates, writes some half-hearted sen-
      tences.

204. Tuuli is very tired. The hour hand on the watch face
      nears 21.00, and then suddenly 22.00.

205. Tuuli scours passages. Re-reads them over and over
      looking for key words. She has run out of time to read
      closely.

206. Tuuli presses her fingers against more keys on the key-
      board, for longer times. The words cohere less and
      less. The words on the screen appear at a distance.
      It is 23.00. She misses a premise; she finds unneeded
      repetition in wording; she sees a misspelling; she sees
      another. It all jumbles together. What's her objection?
      She doesn't know. This isn't her sort of thing. She isn't
      the kind of thing that does this. She *just is* the kind of
      thing that wonders. *There's a way in which* she might be
      more than just a thing that wonders, but she can't be
      sure even by a conventional string of words. It is 00.00.

207. Tuuli's thoughts wander. Blurry pictures form and turn inside out and move through and around words. The white background of the document on which she writes her paper looks more colorful now. And the later it gets, the less she understands what she has written.

208. Tuuli repeats herself. She thinks: Elämin-niin-kausik-kat tarvea yksiavastiset, laula, kilpikonna. That looks like it could be meaningful Finnish. Parts of it are. Most isn't. But it looks like it could be. It seems like I could speak Finnish, though probably not to Finns.

209. Tuuli bites her lip. Hyvä ystäväni. "You'll never see her again. You love her: You love Maiju."

210. Tuuli's thoughts turn. She wonders if she's doing the right thing, if university is good for her. If philosophy is good for her. Anthropology certainly wasn't. Math or physics, perhaps that is what it is. To be ordered by quantities. That is what she should do, she thinks, or rather, that is what she *should* have done or should be doing. She should be doing something sensible, some-thing associated with practical application. Engineer-ing, perhaps? She thinks: Can I still? It is stressful to come to think that explanations in natural language can't describe all the parts of reality adequately…at least they don't seem to be able to. Even if they could, would that help me? You can't be helped. And what do

I have left without them? What does philosophy do for me? The descriptions of reality that matter are so greatly removed from everyday language and experience... one can just emote the feelings of doing math in physics, and this is the closest a person can come to grasping anything about the fundamental structure of reality. Does this surprise you though? I have to be sad that I don't *understand*, and moreover, that I don't even know what I don't understand, and it feels hopeless. Tuuli thinks: En ymmärrä. Could I at least have my beloved Suomi? This is why Einstein must have been such a determined determinist. We can't but see comprehensible succession; our apparatus organizes whatever it reacts with in this way. Then how— the supposed paragon of our organized endeavors, mathematics, through physics—how can it have led us into an incomprehensible world?

Tuuli thinks—

How does mathematics match up against reality? I locate that as important. I don't even know how to go about beginning to assess that, though—I just want to know. Maybe then it will be clear how quantum mechanics relates to reality. But you can't really think quantum mechanics has it right—surely that wave will collapse? It could just be another misguided amalgam of the mistakes of whatever biological phenomenon reason amounts to. Well, that's dumb. But you're not dumb for thinking it. But you are dumb for thinking that.

Stop halting yourself and let your mind drift the course. I cannot even address these possibilities. They are probably formulated terribly in my own thoughts anyway. Besides, I know nothing about these matters. How can I find them compelling? But I do. Does it matter if I am wrong? Does it matter if I have them wrong? I still have the feelings I have, and those feelings are better when they are feelings that seem to be, if nothing else at all, interacting in some way with the furthest ideas I can reach from the confines of the meager capacity that I have been afforded. Though perhaps the feelings would be richer if I knew more. I have nothing much to work with here, but in my own fleeting and stupid self-organizing, I suppose it matters more to feel as I do in the times that I feel the ways I like to. There is some special harmony about the inarticulate chasm that lies beyond wondering, where an answer would be, and *that* that chasm is there, *knowing* that it is, is perhaps enough for me as long as I hold the thought in my head. That's where the suchness is going to be.

211. Tuuli can tell she is tired. Her eyes ache, her temples throb. When she begins to think haphazardly beyond her comfortable grasp, her uncertainty leads her to confuse herself. Then again, she thinks, I am confounded at butterflies.

212. Tuuli has already lost sight of the harmony of the chasm, or whatever it was, that she had been thinking just moments ago. Her thoughts turn again. She thinks of thoughts. She wonders what it is to be intelligent, or to be very intelligent, and how that must look. You just have to have the right kind of authentic and eccentric character. But you are so limited, and so frustrated by your own limitedness.

213. Tuuli knows now that she is sleepy. Her thoughts are warm and cozy. Fuzzy. Fluffy. Cloud-like things; she has her head in the air, in the stars, in the clouds. Like Aristophanes' Socrates. She descends from the clouds to wonder about things with whatever apparatus she is. It is more confusing at night. The words are less clear, less concise, and yet more evocative. This isn't better or worse, it is merely a fault of style.

214. Tuuli looks at her watch. It is now 01.56.

215. Tuuli thinks: Why is it so easy to sleep when I have work to be done? Why is it my work that has to be done instead of someone else's? Why didn't I do it earlier? It would have been better. Why don't I do it now? It would be okay. It will be okay. I hope it will.

216. Tuuli thinks: Perhaps I will do better next time.

217. Tuuli thinks: Perhaps I will do better.

218. Tuuli thinks: Perhaps I will.

219. Tuuli thinks: Perhaps.

220. Tuuli sleeps.

About the Author

Steven Nathan McGannon grew up in the redwood forests of Aptos, California.

He began writing stories when he was 3 years old and hasn't yet stopped.

In his spare time, he studies philosophy and anthropology at the University of California, Berkeley.

Please direct any questions or comments to
snmcgannon@gmail.com